D0241619

Assalamu Alaykum

Author **M S Kayani**

Illustrated by Terry Norridge-Austen

THE ISLAMIC FOUNDATION

Assalamu Alaykum!
Here is a new book for you to read.
You will enjoy it, *insha'Allah*.
The book tells you how you can live in peace
and happiness; how to greet your parents,
your brothers and sisters, your friends, your
teachers and everyone you meet.
Every time you use this greeting you will be
doing the same as Prophet Muhammad
(peace be upon him).

Muslims pray for peace for all people, animals and plants.
"We live in peace with them all, *insha' Allah*," says
Abdullah.
"Yes, we are Muslims and want to live in peace
with everyone," says Aminah.

All Muslims are like one big family. They love each other and are kind to each other. They pray for their Muslim brothers and sisters.

"When we meet other Muslims we say, '*Assalamu Alaykum*' to them," says Aminah.

"It means 'peace be upon you'!" says Abdullah. Muslims say *Assalamu Alaykum* when they leave each other as well.

"When I say, '*Assalamu Alaykum*' to Aminah,"
says Abdullah.
"I say '*Wa Alaykum Assalam*' back to Abdullah,"
says Aminah.
This means 'and peace be upon you too.'

This is like a prayer to Allah, to ask Him to bless each other, to bring peace so that we are happy. We like being Muslims because Islam helps us every day.

In the morning, when we wake up, we should say,
'*Assalamu Alaykum*' to our Mum and Dad
and our brothers and sisters.

"When we do, they all say, '*Wa Alaykum Assalam*' back to us," says Aminah.

"We all love each other, so we begin each day with the greeting of peace," says Abdullah.

"When Dad leaves the house he calls out,
'*Assalamu Alaykum*' to us," says Abdullah.
"And we reply, '*Wa Alaykum Assalam*' to him," says
Aminah. Peace be with you, and peace be with you too!

"We both love Dad, so we pray to Allah to bless him,"
say Abdullah and Aminah.
"And Dad loves us too, so he prays to Allah
to bless us as well."

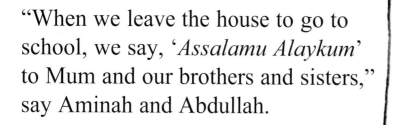

"When we leave the house to go to school, we say, '*Assalamu Alaykum*' to Mum and our brothers and sisters," say Aminah and Abdullah.

"And I reply, '*Wa Alaykum Assalam*' to them," says Mum.
Peace be with you all,
and peace be with you too!

"When we come back from school,
we greet everyone with, '*Assalamu Alaykum*'
as we go into the house," says Abdullah.

"And everyone inside says '*Wa Alaykum Assalam*' back to us," says Aminah.
Peace be with you all, and peace be with you too!

Muslims always say '*Assalamu Alaykum*' when they meet or leave each other. We always pray for each other and wish each other peace and happiness.

"We do this because our Prophet, peace be upon him, did it, and we follow his way," says Aminah.

"This is our way, the Way of Peace, because we are Muslims," says Abdullah.

Prophet Muhammad, peace be upon him, said, "When you enter a house say, '*Assalamu Alaykum*' because this will bring peace to everyone."

He also said, "When you enter any place say, '*Assalamu Alaykum*'."

The Prophet also said, "When you meet anyone, if you know him or not, say, '*Assalamu Alaykum*'."
Peace be with you, and peace be with you too!

"*Assalamu Alaykum*," say Abdullah and Aminah, "and thank you for reading our book."